Text copyright © 2013 by Harriet Ziefert Illustrations copyright © 2013 by Todd H. Goldman
All rights reserved/CIP data is available. Published in the United States in 2013 by
Blue Apple Books, 515 Valley Street, Maplewood, NJ 07040
www.blueapplebooks.com
First Edition 04/13
Printed in China

ISBN: 978-1-60905-363-5

10 9 8 7 6 5 4 3 2 1

Bear in Underwear
Goodnight Underwear

pictures by **Todd H. Doodler**

BLUE APPLE

In a great green forest
There was a little cabin
And a nice campsite
And a campfire
And—

There were seven friends in underwear

And seven bags for sleeping there

And seven pillows on the beds
For seven friends to rest their heads

And seven flashlights on the ground
For seven friends circling round

And spray for ticks and marshmallows on sticks

And a bear in underwear, good at tricks

Goodnight
pillow fight

Goodnight
mosquito bites

Goodnight frights
Goodnight lights

Every friend is tucked in tight

It should be a quiet night

Hello owl's whoo-whoo-whoo
Hello dove's coo-coo-coo

Hello mice running by

Hello—**ouch!**
bug in the eye!

Hello lump
under Bear's back

Hello frog
in Bear's sack

Hello itches
Hello twitches

Hello dark shadows and—what's that sound?

Hello scary thunder and rain pouring down

Hello dry cabin…with friends together

Hello safe from stormy weather

Goodnight glitches
Goodnight twitches

And lots and lots of little itches

Goodnight moon

Goodnight raccoon

Goodnight peepers

Goodnight sleepers

Goodnight little house

Goodnight little mouse

Goodnight dimming lights
Goodnight nighttime frights

Goodnight to undies mighty fine
They are drying on the line

Goodnight to an underwear-ing bear

Goodnight, goodnight,
underwear!